Anomalous Press | Providence, Rhode Island | 2019

The first three unedited fragments/chapters of *Naty and My Chaotic Stench* appear in the limited edition *Witch Fingers* anthology, published by Xander Marro's DMNS Press. Providence, RI. 2013.

Naty And My Chaotic Stench by Shey Rivera Ríos

© 2019

First edition.

ISBN: 978-1-939781-43-7

Designed by Erica Mena. Printed and bound by Bookmobile.

Cover designed and carved by Andrea Perez Bessin

& letterpress printed by Erica Mena.

www.anomalouspress.org

Acknowledgements:

Thank you to my mother Edna Rios and my father Samuel Rivera, for their light, strength, resilience, and love.

Thank you to Nancy, the person who inspired this book and was part of my adolescence. And to her son Adolfo, rest in power and peace.

Thank you to Xander Marro, Sussy Santana, Erica Mena, and Seth Tourjee, for believing in this book and supporting its materialization.

This book is dedicated to the people of Puerto Rico and its diaspora. May our stories live and thrive, standing the test of time.

"jíbara bruja"

Soy bruja
witch that perches on avocado trees
with *talones de gallina de palo*.

Talons of an iguana slowly climbing branches to get a taste of our fruit.

Talons of a rooster trained to fight to defend my honor.
I am most comfortable under the rainstorms that make the montes sweat
and birth streams.

I can see that you have

eyes of *el guaraguao* (the hawk) as it soars with its kind over mountains,
ears of *el mucaro* (the owl) listening to the rustle of palm trees.

The skirts of the island have been lifted
and a leather belt has licked her skin, left trails of red, blue, black
to replace our flag.

This is a funeral.

With all its intricate ornaments and multicolored blossoms,
it is still a funeral.

My *jíbara* spirit is a magnetic field
cradled in the plantain breasts of the forest.

I can only follow its call.

It sounds like thunder and rides the back of wild horses.
    Yes, we've got wild horses.

Tell me,
where are you from?

Did you get here on purpose?

Where are you headed?

What are your dreams made of?
Mine taste like rain.

NATY AND MY CHAOTIC STENCH

Darkness. A purple haze. The oracle speaks….

Once was red and twice was crimson blood. Tonight prophetic visions echo from my pillows. In exchange for a bag of sleep-leaves, I shall reveal the movement of the planets by reading the way blood rushes through my veins. From underneath a blindfold, I will share with you a kaleidoscopic vision of reality.

Let's begin...

A huge cigar hangs from her mouth. The room is thick with the scent of paprika, cilantro, and tomato sauce. Big buttocks sway under a large purple skirt that sweeps the floor. She's singing one of those *cantinero* songs, from old jukeboxes in Mexican bars. The hexes that rough-looking men sang to their lovers with drunken passion and despair. I sat at the table, planted my black sneakers firmly on the ground, and picked at the chipped black nail polish on my nails.

Fire the casserole *con to y la madre, como dicen por ahí... Pa los gustos, los colores.*

I. Ali

A tangled, hairy mess lays on the bed, arms spread out and legs up on the wall. Long dark hair spilling from the bed to the floor. The Hanged Man. "What a world, what a world...," the wicked witch shrieks out of the television as she melts. I stare at the white paint bubbles on my ceiling. The biggest one takes the shape of South America, dripping out of the dirty, white ceiling. I fantasize about being a wild Amazon woman with hair reaching down to my thighs and wild orchids tangled in unruly curls that smell of waterfalls and mud, rain and mangos, and blossoming Birds of Paradise. Worrying only about the rain.

Smoke from the burning sage gathers into thick blankets above the bed, soundproofing my room so the thunder and the lightning only resonate in my head. I stay quiet and visualize the storm soaking everything up, washing off the colors and wrapping the world in a monochrome blanket. I lick my lips. Peppermint incense makes me hungry...

Music: "Las sirenas" by Los Espíritus, Puerto Rico, 2016.
https://losespiritus.bandcamp.com/track/las-sirenas

II. The Stench

At the moment, I have an urgent matter to resolve. No, let me explain. In these past few weeks, I've started to notice something quite embarrassing: I have acquired an insistent body odor. It's a kind of syrupy, rancid smell. I shower everyday, I swear! I have no idea why this is happening. The people I've asked claim that they can't smell a thing, but they might be lying; the type of nice that will not get its hands dirty.

In the Department Store, I slip between perfume booths without uttering a single sound, avoiding eye contact with the saleswomen and their overly done makeup. I cruise around the aisles, sliding through thick clouds of Chanel and Yves Saint Laurent and all those other tiny bottles I can't afford, desperately searching for a magic potion that could hide my persistent odor. But, like a curse, all scents merged into a single odor—a knife that slowly pierced my nostrils—and I could no longer tell the difference. It was a smell that reminded me of the slow plastic decay of ladies with Botox and lots of jewelry. "Frustration" was scribbled like an invisible tattoo on my forehead. I could feel it; it itched. What a total waste of time. This chaotic stench was still following me...

I need to talk to Naty.

III. Esoteric coffee

Pouring Coffee sound effect:
https://www.youtube.com/watch?v=SuL9PoaGbuY

I have to tell you about my friend Naty.

Naty is a 42 year-old Puerto Rican with big red lips, green *ojos brujos*, *café con leche* skin, and hair dyed *colorao' profundo*.

She is always *mandando pa buen sitio a su* sixteen year-old son. "*¡Me dan ganas de mandarte con esto a la cabeza, tan fácil como chuparme un limber!*" she screams at him as she waves an enormous raspberry-scented candle in a heavy glass container. Gilberto just rolls his eyes. There's nothing like the bond between mother and son.

Naty will soon be crowned as a *santera*. She's a daughter of Oshún, the river goddess, the queen of honey and love. However, Naty *si que tenía mala suerte* in the love department. But nowadays days, *quién no*, right?

Naty survives on a social security check, tarot readings, magic potions and *baños*, and rituals for her recurring clientele, including angry and love-sick women, unfaithful cops of all genders, and desperate individuals looking to get their loved ones out of jail.

She does her readings in her living room. Everything in this room is peach, white, and gold. She collects anything angel-related: paintings, *figuras*, wallpaper, coasters, *muñecas*, you name it. *Esa manía kitsch que tiene la gente aquí; cachibaches, embelecos.* The room was furnished with two loveseat sofas with fancy cushions and a chair covered with a cloak of goat fur. Every piece of furniture was covered with porcelain dolls; blonde angels that listened attentively to everything uttered in the room, observing through big glass eyes that lurked behind perfect curls.

Naty served my coffee and sat down at her reading table. She took out a cherry cigar and lit it as she puffed out the smoke with her big, red lips. She opened a bottle of rose water, poured a bit on her hand and rubbed her palms. She sprinkled some on her tarot deck as she mumbled prayers.

The smoke she exhumed circled around her as she dealt her tarot deck. She placed the cherry of the cigar inside her mouth, without burning her tongue, and puffed smoke onto her deck. Smoke offered for the *santos* and the *muertos*.

Naty whispered smoky prayers as she motioned with her hands, smoothing down the fly-aways of her aura and making the surrounding smoke ripple like eager spirits.

A Hawaiian tune starts playing. Steel drums and surf sounds interrupt the ritual. She answers her phone. *"Alo? Sí, ya lo tengo preparao. Vamos a brujearle a ese hijo de la gran yegua."* You could feel the heat blowing out of her mouth like a dragon as she spoke on her cell phone. She was talking with a customer for whom she had finished a *trabajo*. "*Vamos a* hex that son of a bitch." She had an accent, but her English was ok. "*Te quiero, mamita. Dios te cuide.*" She hung up.

Naty had that maternal and authoritative vibe exuded by matriarchal women; a promise of embrace and protection, like a river goddess mother. She was a woman who had lived an intense life. Divorced twice and had many failed love affairs. She had two sons, each from a different father. The eldest one married young due to an early pregnancy, turning Naty into a young *abuela* with a cute, three year-old *nieto*. "*Ese nene es el diablo; mi adoración,*" she said as she showed me the most recent picture of her wild yet lovable grandson with his messy red curls and freckled cheeks.

Gilberto was her youngest son. *Un caco*, a reggaeton scenester. He was really into his car, like most *chamaquitos* from around here. It was a red 1991 Isuzu Trooper, with a loaded stereo system and extra lights in creative places inside the car. He planned to add huge decals of Japanese robots to his *guagua*.

"*Deja de ser tan vago y ve a comprar leche. ¡Pero que no te quedes una hora y me traigas la leche cortá!! ¡Ven derechito pa' acá!*"

As he left to buy milk at the *colmado* down the street, Naty resumed her reading ritual and began the spread. Five cards on the table: Two above, one in the middle, and two below. More were added downward from the top, forming three columns as the cards revealed visions to the redhead reader...

Ay Eleguá, ábreme los caminos...

IV. El Mercado

Naty gave me another list of ingredients for another one of her herbal remedy baths, a *despojo*. I'm a bit tired of these and of spending money. I mean, I can find a few of her ingredients in the backyard and in her kitchen, but I have to go to *el mercado* because she doesn't let me use her supplies. "*Pues* that's my business, *mija*. You're already getting it all *gratis*!", she yells nonchalantly as she turns toward her stove and waves her wooden spoon. Not sure how much of a remedy they are anyway. The smell goes away for a few minutes and then comes back. Ugh.

I drive over to *el mercado* with a list of ingredients to prepare the *despojo*:

Ruda / Rue
Yerba Buena / Spearmint
Esencia de Abre Caminos / Open Roads essence
Canela / Cinnamon
Manzanilla / Chamomile
Pétalos de rosa / Rose petals
Clavos / cloves
Agua Florida / Florida Water

V. Doña Silva and the cemetery of cigarettes

Music: "Oigo voces" by Mima, Puerto Rico, 2011.
Written by Rita Indiana.
https://www.youtube.com/watch?v=Zy1cQwxUoLM

Its 3:00 pm. On one of the many hot and slow afternoons that are only brightened by the occasional breeze.

Doña Silva is Naty's *maestra*, her teacher of *la obra*. We drove in spirals over and around two *montes* to get here. Naty parked her car under a large palm tree. We entered through a red concrete fence, framed by two columns with two sculptures of white, impish boys sitting on koi fish.

We passed by the terrace and approached a shed with a small porch. An old man was sitting impatiently. A holographic image of the Holy Heart hung from the door of the shed. This was the room of the *consultas*. The door was closed.

"You go in after the *señor*."

"Are you sure?"

"Yes, you go first."

I rested against the wall and looked to the floor. I noticed the cement floor outside the shed was covered with cigarette butts and small seashells. Naty soon contributed to the cigarette cemetery, as she flicked hers off with her acrylic nails. Its ember faded out against the seashells and its last breath of smoke faded into nothingness.

There was a small fountain next to the gate, in a small patch of soil and greenery. I reached out to pick up a shell.

"Don't touch that".

The fountain was small with natural rocks glued on cement, surrounding a one-foot tall Virgin Mary statue, with rosary in hand and the trademark blue shroud, as well as the snake between her feet.

I fantasized about Mary being alive in the contemporary world; she could be a B-girl. Blue hoodie and bling rosary, making Hallelujahs fierce and warm like a Gospel singer. An earth-colored girl with no papers. Or she could be a punk with a halo caught in her nose, a snake tattooed around her ankle, and blue hair shrouding her face. She would spit at people who dared to judge her sexual identity.

The Sacred Heart door opened and a teenage girl walked out, followed by a woman in her 40s. After them, an older woman appeared in a floral dress, emitting a squeal through her thin lips:

"Cójelo con calma mija, no te dejes coger de pendeja. Los hombres son como los chavos prietos: Ya no valen ni pa' dulces."

"Take it easy, don't let yourself be fooled. Men are like pennies, not even worth enough for candy."

The old woman looked intently at me, like a cop. Then, a thin-lipped smile crept through her mouth. It turned into a grin, with missing teeth, a few yellow ones and a gold plated fang. I smiled back but couldn't hide my awe at the glimmer in her mouth. She quickly turned to face the old man that was waiting for her:

"Bueno mijo, vamos a lo mismo. When will you learn?" She had a heavy Cuban accent.

"Bueno, Señora, así están las cosas. Por eso vengo pa' acá," he replied, half embarrassed.

They walked into the room and closed the door. Another cigarette leaped off the edge of Naty's acrylic claws. It joined the other brown corpses in their cement graveyard with seashell tombstones.

We waited. 20 minutes. My phone had low battery.

The old man emerged from the room carrying a bottle filled with a dark liquid, branches, and leaves. He turned to face Doña Silva, his hand rose to draw the sign of the cross on his forehead and chest.

Doña Silva floated toward me and grabbed my wrist. She had black cat claws. Her natural nails, long, black, sharp. She gently turned my wrist on its vulnerable side. Smelled it. "Follow me".

The room. It was an altar. You were immediately caught in the aura of a large, ceramic Saint Lazarus, surrounded by flowers, candles, horseshoes, a cauldron, a sword, smaller statues of other saints. There was only space left for a bed and a chair. A large glass vase with water and herbs rested on the floor, next to the bed. The door closed behind us.

VI. The Tunnel of Trees // Xiomara in Blue

This is a car drive, a forest ride; a road to the other side. It doesn't even need to be a secret; no one ever pays much attention. Somehow, they don't realize it. I took it.

I took the road. A tunnel of trees, desolate daytime.

After many rough breaths, my fatigued car stopped.

I decided to walk.

A girl dressed in a light blue *quinceañera* dress and two of her friends appeared from the trees. They were blue bells, ringing with voices like sparkling glass.

"*Hola, soy Xiomara. Es mi quinceañero.* And I wanted to see the road no one walks on," she chirped. They danced and ran away, toward the mouth of the tunnel. Their images blurred like static from a video tape.

> "*Que te beso las manos*
> *Y te miro guiando*
> *Y tu amor nos hizo un ofrenda*"

My body turns on the warm trap that is my bed. My eyes hungry for light but hurting, they reach for the window. Grey Kingbirds are making a nest on the lime tree. They will now attack anyone who passes under it.

> *"Comprendo que era yo, que era yo, y que era yo- la sombra!"*
> Music: "Sueño", by La Lupe, 1969. Cuba.
> https://www.youtube.com/watch?v=re4DSWDzdic

The song ends, gives way to roosters clawing at the morning.

My legs slide off the bed. Feet slide into the kitchen. A kettle with water, set on the stove. Stove lit. Sage burning. I bounce back to bed with a skull mug that Naty had given me as a gift.

Text message from Abey. His band plays tonight and he offered a ride to the show. Abey is the vocalist and guitarist in a punk band called Sagaz. He is *indio*, with *piel canela* and long, straight black hair. A slick crooner. Abey was not born male, but he is. We've been friends for three years; he's obnoxious, but charming enough to get away with it.

Flash forward to the show: Plaid skirts and fishnets, vintage dresses and glasses, doc martens and runny mascara. Clouds of dust rising from under worm-out, buckled boots. Leather and cigarettes, smoke. Dust.

After the fourth song, my chest began pounding hard and I could barely breathe. I slithered away to catch some fresh air. Found some steps on the building next to the venue. The night breeze cooled my face.

I moved my foot and knocked something over. A CD player. How old is this? I quickly took the headphones and hit play. A band I've never heard before. No vocals. All electronic; it made me think of a fluorescent bay; dark, smooth, and electric.

Someone tapped my shoulder. I took off the headphones.

"That's mine." A grin bloomed on thick purple lips releasing cigarette smoke.

VII. Black Rabbit

"Will you steal it?"

"I haven't seen one of these in years"

The grin faded into a smile, leaving room for me to notice their bright black eyes.

"I'm Lo"

"Ali. *Mucho gusto.*"

Abey burst out the door. His big smile eroded into a scowl.

"Hey! Were you outside all this time? I was hoping you'd stay for the set..."

"Hello," greeted Lo, with their big smile.

"Qué hay," puffed Abey.

"I caught your set. It sounded great." I reluctantly tried to comfort Abey.

"Yea, cool."

Abey moved past us to join a crowd outside.

"Do you two know each other?" I asked.

"We went to the same high school. Used to be close. Things got messy though," Lo laughed and flicked their cigarette into the street. It faded like a settling firefly.

"What happened?"

"You ask too many questions. That gets people in trouble," Lo smirked.

I looked at my broken cell phone to check on the time. "See you around," Lo gave a slight bow before disappearing into the crowd of bronze punks cackling out in the *pastizal*.

X. El curandero // The Witch Doctor

Don Alvin was an old *curandero*, a healer, that lived *en las parcelas*, (the parcels) in the mountains. He has white hair and a thick white mustache. He wore old polo shirts, long pants, a baseball cap, and the traditional beaded necklaces of the orishas. His clothes were usually old and a bit dirty.

One afternoon, as I was leaving Naty's house, this old man arrived to see her. He met my gaze straight on, locked on me as I got into my car. Once I started my engine, I found him standing in front of my car, motioning me to get out: *"Tu te me bajas ahora."* I turned off the car and opened my door. "Have you been in a car accident recently?", he asked with a fierce gaze. "Actually, I've had two this week", I replied with what I'm sure was a wide-eyed response. *"¡Ay, si tu te me vas a la tercera!"* ("Oh, they will get you the third time!")

We went inside Naty's house, but this time he was the one conducting the ritual. He pulled out a spray can with a label that depicted Archangel Michael defeating the demon. "Lucky, I brought this! I knew it was odd that something was telling me to bring it with me today." He asked me to lay down on the floor face down. He sprayed my back with the magic spray can; then he held my arms and stepped on my back.

"Have you been having back pains?" he asked, sounding like a cryptic commercial.

"Yes, she's been looking like a hunchback girl lately", Naty replied as she fanned herself with a celebrity gossip magazine. She was sipping cheap beer from a straw, her red lipstick stamped on the plastic.

I had no time to get angry; I was too preoccupied wailing at every electric shock that was sent up my spine with every step that Don Alvin took on my back.

"There! ¡*Como nueva!* Good as new!", he yelled.

"*¡Mira pá 'llá! La nena* can stand straight now!" Naty chimed in.

"Let's get ready *pá abrir la mes*a. That is, Naty, if you don't mind," said Don Alvin.

"Not at all, you can go ahead," Naty said as she turned around and headed back to the kitchen. Don Alvin took a cigar out from his chest pocket and lit it. He puffed for a few minutes. "Give me your left hand." I followed orders. He grabbed my hand with his cold, old, and dark hand. His nails were at least an inch long. With the cigar backwards into his mouth, he puffed a cloud of smoke that swallowed my hand. As the cloud vanished, he kept staring into my left palm. His eyes kept an intense purpose. His lips pursed.

"*Te han estao trabajando.* You have a *trabajo*, a spell, that has been planted on your back, to see you in a hospital. It's like a shadow of a palm tree planted on your back".

"Someone experienced is involved, someone who is targeting Naty. An attack on your *madrina* has reflected onto you."

"*¡¿Que qué?!* That filthy *víbora*! She's playing with me!" Naty shrieked. "*Mira y que* messing with my Alicia! She's messing with *fuego del malo! ¡No sabe lo que le viene!*"

Don Alvin tried to calm down Naty. "Don't worry. Drop by my house tomorrow. I have snake oil and a few other things. Naty, bring a bead necklace for her, so we can break this."

The next day, Naty took me to Don Alvin's house. After some narrow roads in the mountain, we parked next to an *Alelí* tree. A stone path led to a driveway, down a hill, where his house emerged from the trees. He had two sheds, similar to Doña Silva's except they didn't have a waiting area. One was locked with chains and the paint was coming off. The other was painted light blue and had a wooden cross hanging from the door.

I wore an old white t-shirt, old jeans, and white underwear, no bra, like Naty asked me to. Don Alvin had many useful trees and herbs growing around his house.

Mejorana / Marjoram,
Ruda / Rue,
Albahaca / Basil,
Artemisia / Wormwood,
Cundeamor / Bitter Melon,

and many others. All of which he would use for baths and rituals.

He led us through a path to the right of his house that continued down the hill and led to an unfinished bathroom on the side of the foundation of his house. As he walked, he took some leaves off one of the trees. We entered a room that was raw concrete, the bare bones of a room. It was empty, but had a make-shift shower. Its likely that Don Alvin was building out this part of he house by himself.

He lit candles and asked me to take my pants off and get in the shower. He picked up what looked like a bucket of herbal water, a ritual bath, that he had prepared prior to our arrival. He lit a cigarette and kept it between his pursed lips. He began chanting a prayer as he dumped a first round of cold, aromatic water on me, catching me by surprise with a painful chill.

"Ay!! This is so cold!"

"Shusshhh!", Naty snapped.

Don Alvin now took me by the shirt and ripped it. He took the pail and dumped more of the herbal water on me. He chanted louder and louder. I gasped for air. He took out a strange bottle with yellowish-brown liquid. "This is snake oil." He poured it on his hand and asked me to turn around. Naty gave him the bead necklace he had requested. He smeared the oil with an open palm over my naked back and held the necklace with the other hand, as he clenched his fist. His palm and fist both pressed in strong pulses on my shoulder blades and my spinal cord. I felt like I was caught in a current, paralyzed. Once more, he dumped the last of the herbal water on my back. Don Alvin flicked his cigarette into the jungle that crept down that hill. My long hair, now wet, clung to my body. I'm shivering. Naty handed me a towel, and fresh clothes.

I remember walking from *el rancho* back to my house at night, past the tangerine tree. I was carrying my music equipment. I was carrying too much, so I decided to turn around. I looked toward the curve. And there, next to the tangerine tree, stood a glowing figure of a girl with curly, black hair, wearing a white dress. Am I imagining things? I felt dizzy, so I turned back around and carried the equipment back home, up the hill. I looked back once I reached the gate. The figure had disappeared.

XI. Vientos

I received a phone call from Naty. I drove that evening to her house and parked my car near the white gate that lined her home. Walked into the terrace and stepped through the door to her kitchen. About 10 people sat in her kitchen and living room. Naty had an open coconut on one hand, Florida water on the other, a kerosene can under her arm, and a cigar on her mouth. She walked onto the terrace, poured kerosene inside the coconut and placed it on the floor. Then, she lit her cigar and turned its cherry toward the inside of her mouth so she could blow smoke onto every person as they formed a circle around her. She lit the coconut on fire. Each of us walked clockwise around the coconut as part of the cleansing ritual, our arms motioning from head to toe as if we were undressing from layers of skin. The fire grew. It turned into a whirl of embers that reached my height. It kept spiraling for about 10 minutes then, quickly, the coconut swallowed it. That month I had recurring dreams of heavy winds.

XII. Nothing

Llego a la casa y me pongo a fumar
con mis dedos de hielo.
Con tanto frío que tengo se me ha espantado
hasta el miedo.
Music: "Heroes del Estereo," by Huáscar Robles.
Puerto Rico. 2010.

Neither Naty, nor Dona Silva, nor Don Alvin could figure this out. The stench still follows me like a *muerto* hiding in the corners. Naty taught me to leave small white plates with peppermint bon bons on a corner of the room. "The rats won't touch them, trust me. Those are for Elegua, who lives in corners and crossroads. And an upside down jar of water on top of the refrigerator to keep the *muertos* and the past lovers away." I lit *palo santo* and placed it next to the jar. These two things must always be kept at a high point of the house. So many rules.

XIII. La citrina / Snake Dream

Eyes open. My limbs swaying in a river. I'm attempting to cross to the other side, but the current is strong. Not strong enough to keep me from moving, I swam diagonally.

Two snakes undulated on the surface by the edge of the water at the other side. One emerald green, the other citrine yellow. They caught the brightness of the sun and turned crystalline.

The citrine noticed me. She began her sway toward me. I tried to turn back, to swim away. But she was a better swimmer and I realized there was no stopping the inevitable. I turned around to face her. Water up filling my mouth. Rushing out my nose. She prepared to strike. I turned to face her. My fist caught her neck in a lock. Her head blossomed into a gaped, bright-pink mouth with two pirite fangs.

Eyes open. I'm in bed. Abey is next to me, a radiator of heat. I stare at the ceiling for a few minutes. The house is quiet, but dawn isn't. The ever echoing chant of the coquis remains sovereign. Roosters call in the morning from a distance, like lovers that don't commit but keep coming back to each other.

The fur blanket slides off my thighs as I slip out of

bed.

Stretch.

Walk to the kitchen.

Fill the kettle with water.

Light the stove.

Brush my teeth.

Sit at the kitchen table and stare at the prayer plant.

Tap long blue nails onto the tarot deck. Take a sip of tea. I pull a single card.

Queen of Cups.

XIX. Gil

Sixteen year old Gilberto had been killed. This was in the news that day. He was with his cousin, who was being chased by the police. They were on their way home from school. And they both got caught in a crossfire. Gilberto's cousin was injured. Gilberto died. Caught in the crossfire.

Naty felt deep guilt. She had agreed to house his cousin for a week, knowing he was evading the police.

Gilberto. Her youngest son… She couldn't handle this loss.

XX. El cementerio

In that neighborhood, El Cuco. It was called that way because they said that at night El Cuco came out from under the mango trees.

It was a hot day out. A clear cerulean sky.

Naty needed to visit the cemetery today.

She needed earth from seven graves, to collect seven warriors for her *caldero*, her cauldron. We took ground *cascarilla*, ground eggshell, and made crosses on our palms, the bottom of our feet, and our heads.

Jekua jey, Oya, baronesa del cementerio. A tu enorme casa no queremos llegar.

Greetings to Oya, baroness of the cemetery. We don't want to stay trapped in your large house.

We walked guided by her palpitations. I walked right behind her, with a metal spoon in hand. She had a bag filled with 7 small glass jars.

Once she picked a grave, she kneeled, prayed. Nothing. She stood up and kept walking. Next one. She kneeled, prayed. Silence. A smile. I handed her the spoon. She whispered a prayer as she took some of the earth next to the tombstone.

We did this until sunset.

That night, Naty had an episode. Her screams flooded the living room at 11pm. They spilled on the floor in pools of shadows. She held on to her voice recorder and insisted she heard conversations. The audio files were just white noise.

XXI. Brujas

Bruja. That means witch in Spanish. When I was younger, my grandma would talk about *las brujas*, who would perch on the trees and steal children.

Brujas climb the trees, they look like hens with feathers gorged on the head, like pom poms. They wipe their beaks between feathers. They pick at the electric cables. Their heels are echos.

In the morning, you can find evidence they were there: a large, fluorescent yellow mushroom grows below the tree where they perched.

XX. The River

Naty. Are you a river? Both in one place and in all places at the same time? You exist in a single fleeting moment and all at once. You flow over things paving paths. You erode, you enrich, you push. Your laughter like rocks and bells, harsh.

Hurricane season. The mountains spill over, noisy and excited. The sky is raging. Avocado trees are birthing like crazy, some of their branches touch the floor. They roll over the hills to rot. This will be a heavy season of storms.

Naty, the streams that bleed out of the mountains are really just you, always on a rush. Will you return to the *madre oceano* or become a lake on your own?

XXII. *Ofrenda*

Another dream. This time, I was nurturing three newborn panthers. Kept them safe on a wooden cage built up on a canopy of mango trees. Safe from predators who wanted to devour them before they fulfilled their power.

It's been three years since I've seen Naty. Her *madrina* told me she moved to Utuado to live by the rivers; that she was called by her mother Oshun to heal, along the riverbed, in the heart of the island.

I remember when Naty and I went to beach with an *ofrenda* one morning, a gift for Yemaya, mother of the sea. The sun felt good on my skin and the breeze cooled the hot earth. All the shades of blue were crisp and clear that day. We brought white wild flowers with us. Facing the ocean, we poured honey over the blossoms, and released them into the tides. Thank you Yemaya. Keep the safety of our family, those of blood and those of spirit.

I've taken on Naty's craft, like she expected I would. *"Tú vas a tomar mi camino, nena. Ya tu versa, fuiste hecha pa' esto. Mejor que yo. Eres más fuerte."*

I accepted this path the day after the rainstorm, after finding Naty's note. The storm seized and the sky was crisp and cerulean.

I was called to the beach that morning.

I walked into the tide and lowered my body onto the water, the skirts of Yemaya. I closed my eyes. Felt warm and held.

That morning, the stench disappeared.

I understood.

Shey Rivera Ríos (pronouns: they/them) is a multi-genre artist and arts manager. They are active in the mediums of performance, installation, digital media, and poetry/narrative. The creations spam several genres and a myriad of topics, from home to capitalism to queerness to magic. Rivera is also a performance curator and producer of interventions that activate people creatively. Participation in national organizations include: member and alumni of the National Association of Latino Arts and Culture (NALAC), member of the Board of Directors of the Alliance of Artist Communities, Fellow of the Intercultural Leadership Institute (ILI) 2017-2018, and Brown University Public Humanities Community Fellow 2017-2019. Rivera has a BA in Psychology and Sociology from the University of Puerto Rico, Rio Piedras campus, and graduate studies in Contemporary Media and Culture from the University of the Sacred Heart, San Juan, Puerto Rico. sheyrivera.com

The twenty-fifth book in the Anomalous Press chapbook series, this book was designed by Erica Mena and the cover designed by Andrea Peres Bessin and letterpress printed by Erica Mena in a limited edition of 100 copies.

Anomalous Press is dedicated to the diffusion of writing in the forms it can take. We're searching for imaginary solutions in this exceptional universe. We're thinking about you and that thing you wrote one time and how you showed it to us and we blushed.

www.anomalouspress.org

Published by **Anomalous Press:**

1. *Courting an Orbit* by Alma Baumwoll

2. *An Introduction to Venantius Fortunatus for Schoolchildren or Understanding the Medieval Concept World through Metonymy* by Mike Schorsch

3. *The Continuing Adventures of Alice Spider* by Janis Freegard

4. *Ghost* by S. Tourjee

5. *Mystérieuse* by Éric Suchère, translated by Sandra Doller
selected by Christian Hawkey

6. *The Everyday Maths* by Liat Berdugo
selected by Cole Swensen

7. *Smedley's Secret Guide to World Literature by Jonathan Levy Wainwright, IV, age 15* by Askold Melnyczuk

8. *His Days Go By The Way Her Years*
by Ye Mimi, translated by Steve Bradbury

9. *Mimi and Xavier Star In A Museum That Fits Entirely In One's Pocket* by Becca Barniskis

10. *Outer Pradesh* by Nathaniel Mackey

11. *The Occitan Goliard Songs of Clamanc Llansana followed by a French prose poem of Marcel de l'Aveugle*
translated and introduced by Kit Schluter

12. *Third Person Singular* by Rosmarie Waldrop

13. *Anatomy of a Museum* by A. Kendra Greene

14. *Drown/Sever/Sing* by Lina Maria Ferreira Cabeza-Vanegas

15. *The All-New* by Ian Hatcher

16. *Book of Interludes* by Grace Shuyi Liew

17. *The Surrender* by Veronica Esposito

18. *Body Split: When Tongue Was Muscle* by S. Tourjee /
I Wanted Just To Be Soft by Temim Fruchter

19. *Cargo* by Pia Deas

20. *The Stone Collector* by A. Kendra Greene

21. *Vagrants & Uncommon Visitors* by A. Kendra Greene

22. *rojo si pudiera rojo // red if it could be red* by Ana Belén López, translated by Ryan Greene

23. *elegía / elegy* by Raquel Salas-Rivera

25. *Naty & My Chaotic Stench* by Shey Rivera Ríos

26. *The Memory of Now* by Geet Chaturvedi, translated by Anita Gopalan

Anthologies:

Come As You Are ed. by E. Kristin Anderson

Puerto Rico en mi Corazón
ed. Erica Mena, Raquel Salas Rivera,
Ricardo Maldonado, Carina del Valle Schorske